Crabapple End

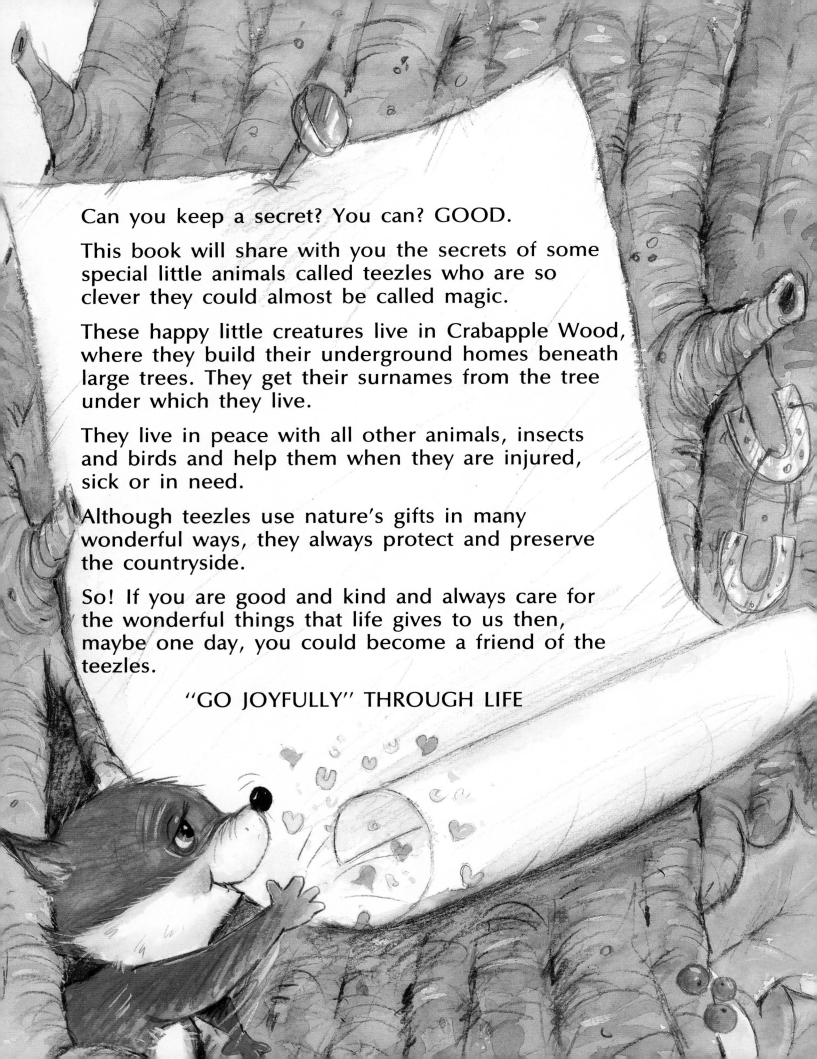

Can you keep a secret? You can? GOOD.

This book will share with you the secrets of some special little animals called teezles who are so clever they could almost be called magic.

These happy little creatures live in Crabapple Wood, where they build their underground homes beneath large trees. They get their surnames from the tree under which they live.

They live in peace with all other animals, insects and birds and help them when they are injured, sick or in need.

Although teezles use nature's gifts in many wonderful ways, they always protect and preserve the countryside.

So! If you are good and kind and always care for the wonderful things that life gives to us then, maybe one day, you could become a friend of the teezles.

"GO JOYFULLY" THROUGH LIFE

THE TEEZLE WEDDING DAY RESCUE

by Terry Barber

Published by Peter Haddock Limited,
Bridlington, England.

© Terry Barber

Illustrated by Wizard Art,
courtesy of Bernard Thornton Artists, London.

THE TEEZLE
WEDDING DAY RESCUE

There was great excitement in Crabapple Wood. A Teezle Wedding had been arranged. Lark Oak was to marry his childhood sweetheart, Fragrance Ash.

All the teezles assembled near a large holly tree where Linden Beech, the chief teezle, stood with the happy couple.

"Lark and Fragrance have decided to build their new home beneath this tree," said Linden, "and I call on you all to follow the teezle tradition and help them. The sooner the work is done, the sooner we can all enjoy a wonderful wedding."

All the teezles cheered and set to work immediately.

The tunnel under the holly tree twisted down through the roots like a helter-skelter and joined the main chamber. From this, passages led to other rooms in the burrow.

Suddenly, there was a shout of excitement from the tunnel and out dashed Clumsy Tub, so named because he was fat and the clumsiest teezle on earth. As he emerged, he tripped and rolled head over heels into a bramble bush. "Ouch," he cried, "I've got prickles in my bottom."

Everyone burst into laughter.

"You can laugh, but I have found treasure," shouted Clumsy Tub, holding up a dirty, black coin. "It must have been lost by the man animals, but it is of no value to us," said Lark.

"Well, I think it's precious and I'm going to show my mother." The fat teezle turned and ran straight into another teezle carrying a load of crabapples. Laughter echoed round the wood once again.

The burrow was soon completed and, on the wedding morning, Lark took Fragrance there to meet his parents, Fern and Silk Oak, to make final arrangements. Just as they arrived Mrs Mouse ran towards them in great distress. "Please help me," she cried. "My son has fallen into a fiendish man animal trap and can't get out."

She led them to a clearing littered with rubbish. A glass jar with particles of food in the bottom had been wedged between two stones. The small mouse lay still, its tiny feet swollen and bleeding. It had obviously clambered into the jar for the food and had not been able to climb out.

The four teezles lifted the jar and gently slid the motionless mouse out on to the grass. "Is he dead?" asked Mrs Mouse tearfully. "No, he's still breathing, but we must get him home quickly," replied Silk. "Why do man animals come into the countryside and spoil the beauty that is theirs to enjoy?" exclaimed Fern angrily as he and Lark gently lifted the tiny mouse.

They carried him back to the oak tree where some of the wedding guests had already arrived. "The wedding will be delayed. A friend is in need of help," explained Fern.

Inside the burrow they treated his injuries and gave him herbal medicine.

"Once he has rested and got over his shock he will be fine," whispered Silk to Mrs Mouse. "You have been very kind. I do hope it has not spoilt your special day," said Mrs Mouse. "Not at all," replied Fragrance. "If he wakes in time, bring him to join in the celebrations."

All the creatures that lived in and around Crabapple Wood had been invited to the wedding. Fragrance looked breathtaking and Lark was very smart in his top hat and tails. Fragrance's best friend, Wren Elm, was the bridesmaid and carried a silk cushion with the wedding ring on it.

They were married by the chief teezle, who placed the gold ring round the tuft on Fragrance's head saying, "You are now Mr and Mrs Holly. May you Go Joyfully through life together."

Then there was a wonderful feast with lots of food and teezle wine. Everyone danced to merry little tunes played by a teezle band.

Clumsy Tub presented them with the coin he had found but, as he did so, he bowed and his trousers, which were far too tight, split at the back, causing great hilarity, much to his embarrassment.

Finally, everyone cheered as the happy couple approached their new home. "Thank you for making our wedding day so happy," said Lark. "Go Joyfully."

They did, especially the little mouse who limped home with his mother.

FAMILY QUEST

Go into a local wood and see how many kinds of tree you can find and identify.

FAMILY QUESTION

What is the average life span of a mouse in the wild?

If you don't know, go to your local library and look for a book to help you find out.